One afternoon, Snake and Bee went to visit Inky. "Come in," Inky welcomed them. "It's such a nice day, so I've put some chairs out in the garden."

As they sat down, Snake noticed a small hedgehog sitting in the middle of the lawn.
"I didn't think hedgehogs came out in the day," said Snake, pointing at it.

“That’s strange,” replied Inky. “It wasn’t there before. It shouldn’t be out in the day. Hedgehogs are nocturnal and normally only come out at night. If you see one out in the day it tends to mean it is ill or in trouble. Let’s go and see if we can help.”

The little hedgehog had its head down and looked like it was asleep. There were also some flies buzzing around it.
"It really does not look very well," said Snake.

"It certainly should not be sitting out like this," said Bee. "I think we should take it to Doctor West's Hedgehog Hospital. She will know how to help it."

Inky went off to get her bike and trailer. Snake got a box, which he lined with newspaper and an old bit of blanket.

"Here we are," he said to the hedgehog. "We are going to get you some help."

They carefully helped the hedgehog into the box, using the bit of blanket to stop the prickles hurting them. Then they loaded the box onto the trailer and Snake tucked the blanket around the hedgehog.

"That should keep you safe and also cosy," he smiled.

Snake sat in the trailer, next to the box, to hold it steady. Inky set off and pedalled her bike as quickly as she could. Bee flew alongside, ready to help if needed.

They soon arrived at Saint Hedgywigs, the Hedgehog Hospital. Doctor West welcomed them in.
"What do we have here?" she said.
Inky explained that they had found the little hedgehog in her garden.

Doctor West peered into the box.
"Oh dear!" she exclaimed. "Yes, indeed, this little hedgehog needs some help quickly. It's not in a good way at all. You did the right thing bringing it here."

Doctor West called one of her nurses to help her, and the nurse took the hedgehog away to the intensive care part of the hospital.

“It’s where we take hedgehogs that need the most help,” she explained.

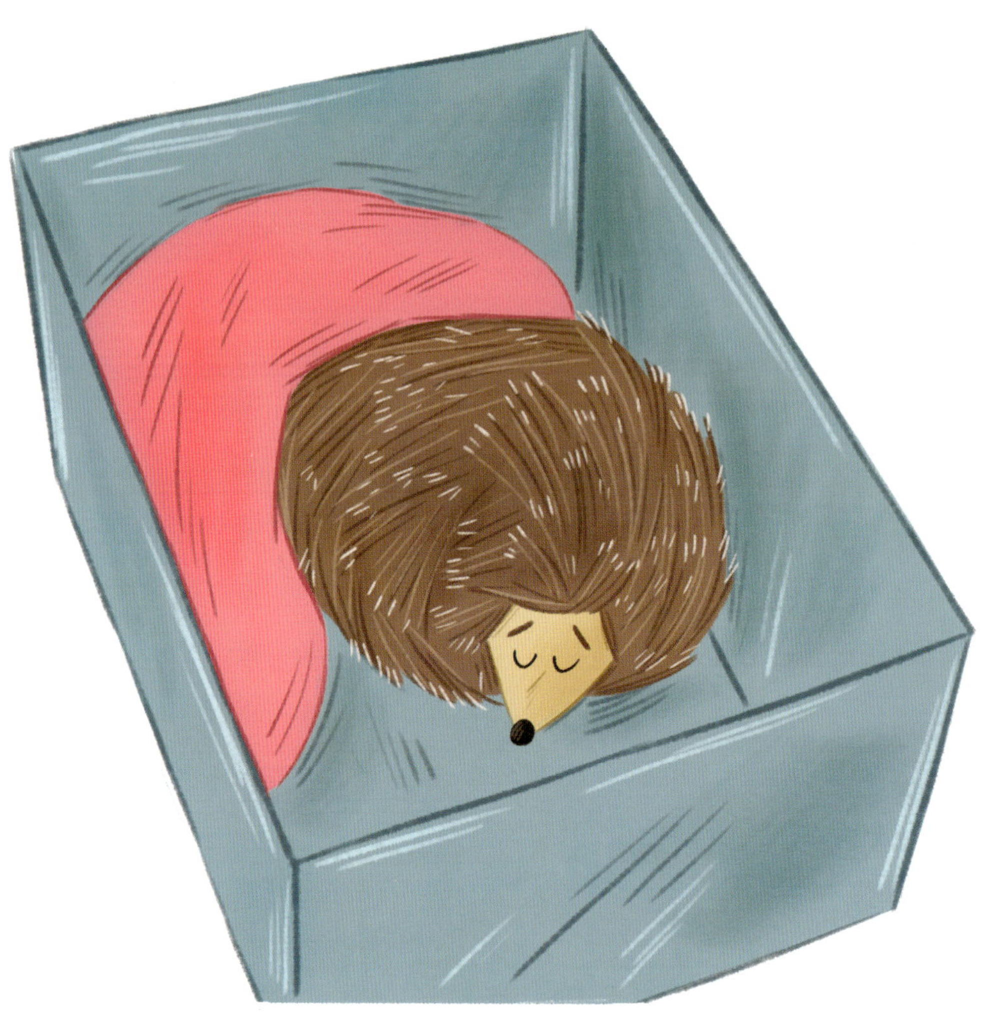

"We will check the hedgehog over and see what help it needs," continued Dr West. "I suspect that it was born late in the year, as it is quite little. It seems a bit cold and is very thin. We will put it on a heat pad and make it snug. Then we will give it something to eat and drink."

"What do hedghogs like to eat?" said Inky. "I heard that they like milk."
"No, you should never give hedgehogs milk, it is not good for their tummies," said Doctor West.

"Hedgehogs eat insects, bugs, slugs, and snails," she continued. "They are sometimes called 'the gardener's friend', as they eat lots of garden pests. Here, however, we feed them meaty dog food," she chuckled.

"Would you like a look around the hospital?" said Doctor West. "I can tell you a bit more about hedgehogs and what we do here at Saint Hedgywigs Hospital."
"We would love that, thank you!" said Inky, Snake, and Bee, and they all went into the hospital together.

"Mostly, hedgehogs hibernate in the winter," explained Doctor West. "They find a sheltered place to curl up and go to sleep. However, they have to be a good size so that they can survive the whole of the winter. I think our little friend must have been struggling to find food."

“We often have a number of little hedgehogs that stay with us over the winter,” said Doctor West. “We provide them with a safe place to live and we feed them. When spring comes, they are bigger and we can release them safely back into the wild.”

“Hedgehogs make nests of leaves in undergrowth, under hedges, sheds, or in other sheltered places,” continued Doctor West. “In the fall, they sometimes try to shelter in piles of wood. You should always check before lighting a bonfire that there are no animals in there.”

“Hedgehogs can curl up into a ball and their sharp spines keep most animals away,” said Doctor West. “They often have a litter of between four and six baby hedghogs in the summer. Baby hedgehogs are called hoglets or urchins.”

"You can help hedgehogs by making a hedgehog house for your garden," said Doctor West. "Put the house in a sheltered part of the garden in a covered spot, so it won't be disturbed. You can put some hay inside for bedding."

"If you put food out for hedgehogs," she continued, "remember to put it away from the hedgehog house, in case other animals are attracted to it. They might disturb any hedgehogs living there."

"Is there anything else we can do to help hedgehogs in our gardens?" inquired Inky.
"Leave a gap under your fence," said Doctor West. "As hedgehogs travel a long way each night looking for food, they need to be able to get from garden to garden."

"What should you do if you have a pond in your garden?" said Bee. "Could they fall in?"
"Surprisingly, hedgehogs can swim very well," said Doctor West, "but you should put in a ramp, so that if they fall in, they can climb out again."

"Well," said Snake. "I didn't know much about hedgehogs this morning, but I do now. We'll come back and check on our little friend over the winter when he is feeling better."
"Yes," said Inky, "we can bring some cans of dog food with us."

"Thank you," said Doctor West, "that would be lovely. Saint Hedgywigs is a charity, so all gifts of food and help are welcome. See you soon!" she called as she waved them goodbye.